Everyone is different, No one's quite the same. This book is all about YOU. What is your name?

For Katie, Alice and Bridie

VIKING
Published by the Penguin Group
Viking Penguin, a division of Penguin Books USA Inc.,
375 Hudson Street, New York, New York 10014, U.S.A.
Penguin Books Ltd, 27 Wrights Lane, London W8 5TZ, England
Penguin Books Australia Ltd, Ringwood, Victoria, Australia
Penguin Books Canada Ltd, 10 Alcorn Avenue, Toronto, Ontario, Canada M4V 3B2
Penguin Books (N.Z.) Ltd, 182–190 Wairau Road, Auckland 10, New Zealand

Penguin Books Ltd, Registered Offices: Harmondsworth, Middlesex, England

First published in Great Britain by William Heinemann Ltd., 1991
First American edition published in 1992

1 3 5 7 9 10 8 6 4 2

Catherine and Laurence Anholt

ALL
ABOUT
YOU

VIKING

When you wake up in the morning, how do you feel?

happy

tired

sad

noisy

quiet

glad

How do you feel today?

When you put on your clothes,

what do you wear?

shoes

shorts

shirt

jeans

sweater

skirt

jacket

underpants

vest

hat

scarf

dress

sandals

socks

suits

T-shirt

tights

boots

What are you wearing now?

When you look out your window, what do you see?

fields

town

sea

city

park   trees

What's outside?

Do you live in a brick house,

or something different?

town house

 castle

 barn

 houseboat

 igloo

 farm

 apartment

 cottage

 greenhouse

 trailer

 tent

 tree house

What's your house like?

Does someone else live with you?

sister   granny   brother

father   baby   mother

Are you feeling hungry?
What do you like?

carrots   cabbage   cheese

pears   pasta   peas

hot dogs   honey   ham

juice   Jell-O   jam

cake

curry

custard

melon

milk

mustard

pancakes

plums

potato

cornflakes

cupcake

cocoa

What's your favorite food?

Do you play with your friends?

jump

skip

chase

trip

fight

race

dance   climb   slide

run   leap   hide

What do you like to play?

Or do you play
on your own?

What do you play with?

bike   drum   train

doll   water   plane

book   ball   puppet

paint   blocks   trumpet

sand   boat   guitar

puzzle   playhouse   car

What's your favorite toy?

Where do you like to go?

party

picnic

pool

zoo

library

school

Which do you like best?

Do you have a special friend?

Or a pet?

What's your favorite animal?

bird

bear

bat

camel

cow

cat

walrus

wolf

whale

sheep

seal

snail

fish

fox

frog

donkey

duck

dog

monkey

mole

moose

gorilla

goat

goose

When it's time for bed, what do you do?

wash   dry   brush

dress   clean up   rush

Everyone is different,
No one's quite alike.
This book was all about you.
Now it's time to say...

GOOD NIGHT.